Have You Seen My Duckling?

Nancy Tafuri

Greenwillow Books · New York

To the little duckling in all of us

Have You Seen My Duckling?
Copyright © 1984 by Nancy Tafuri
All rights reserved.
Manufactured in China by South
China Printing Company Ltd.
www.harperchildrens.com

30 29 28 27 26 25   First Edition

Library of Congress Cataloging-
in-Publication Data
Tafuri, Nancy. Have you
seen my duckling?
"Greenwillow Books."
Summary: A mother duck leads
her brood around the pond as she
searches for one missing duckling.

[1. Lost children—Fiction.
2. Duck—Fiction.
3. Ponds—Fiction.]
I. Title.   PZ7.T117Hav
1984   [E]   83-17196
ISBN 0-688-02797-0
ISBN 0-688-02798-9 (lib. bdg.)
ISBN 0-688-10994-2 (pbk.)

Early one morning...

Have you
seen my
duckling?

Have you
seen my
duckling?

Have
you seen
my duckling?

Have you seen my duckling?

Have you seen my duckling?